CRITICAL THINKING
—— IN ——
AMERICAN HISTORY™

Interpreting America's Civil War

Organizing and Interpreting Information in Outlines, Graphs, Timelines, Maps, and Charts

Therese Shea

The Rosen Publishing Group, Inc., New York

Published in 2006 by The Rosen Publishing Group, Inc.
29 East 21st Street, New York, NY 10010

First Edition

Library of Congress Cataloging-in-Publication Data

Shea, Therese.
Interpreting America's Civil War: organizing and interpreting
information in outlines, graphs, timelines, maps, and
charts/Therese Shea.—1st ed.
     p. cm.—(Critical thinking in American history)
Includes bibliographical references and index.
ISBN 1-4042-0415-6 (library binding)
1. United States—History—Civil War, 1861–1865—Juvenile
literature. 2. United States—History—Civil War, 1861–1865—
Study and teaching (Secondary)—Juvenile literature.
I. Title. II. Series.
E468.S515 2006
973.7—dc22
                                                                    2004030632

Manufactured in the United States of America

On the cover: Left: The Battle of Corinth (Mississippi) in 1862.
Right: The Battle of Gettysburg (Pennsylvania) in 1863.

Contents

The American Civil War

A war between two conflicting groups of citizens in a country is called a civil war. Many countries have experienced civil wars. For most people in the United States, the term "civil war" immediately brings to mind the American Civil War, a conflict fought in the mid-1800s that not only caused much suffering but also resulted in the joy of freedom for former slaves. About 620,000 Americans were killed during the four years of the Civil War. Some of the consequences of the Civil War, such as families

Word Works

The word "civil" is related to the Latin word *civis*, meaning "citizen." A civil war is a war between citizens of a single country. On the Internet or at the library, research other civil wars. Use the outline below as a guide to take notes about two civil wars. Share your findings with another student.

I) First Civil War
   a) Where it took place
   b) Reasons it took place
      i) Details of reason one
      ii) Details of reason two
   c) Results

II) Second Civil War
   a) Where it took place
   b) Reasons it took place
      i) Details of reason one
      ii) Details of reason two
   c) Results

being torn apart by resentment between opposing forces, racial problems, and the destruction of many resources in the Northern and Southern states, are felt even today.

Many people believe the American Civil War was fought over one issue, slavery. Slavery was a major point of disagreement between the Northern and Southern states, although other differences led to the conflict as well. These included disagreements over how much power each state should have as compared to the power of the federal government.

Slavery at the Birth of the Country

The United States of America won its independence from Great Britain in 1783. The representatives of the American people began a difficult task at the Constitutional Convention of 1787. They needed to create a document that would name the powers and duties of the government of their new nation. Nine states were required to ratify, or approve, this document before it could take effect.

The issue of slavery was one of the divisive points between the representatives of the North and South. Although slavery had existed in all the colonies, the system was most common in the South. Some of the Northern states abolished slavery before the Revolutionary War (1775–1783), some after it. Even though the majority of Southerners did not own slaves, the South was heavily agricultural. Tobacco, cotton, and sugarcane crops provided much wealth for the South. The plantations that grew these crops required many laborers. To supply this labor force, plantation owners imported Africans to America as slaves.

Word Works

The word "divisive" means "creating a lack of unity." The prefix "di-" means "two." Think of other words that begin with the "di-" prefix.

A slave family is pictured here in a Savannah, Georgia, cotton field during the 1860s.

Ending slavery in the nation as a whole was never even mentioned at the Constitutional Convention because it was feared that the issue threatened the unity of the nation. Some representatives from both the North and South could not accept the fact that blacks should be considered equal to whites. Many knew that slavery would not last forever and that it was a cruel institution. Thomas Jefferson, a slave owner, said, "Nothing is more certainly written in the book of fate than that these people are to be freed." However, Southern representatives, including Jefferson, believed that the loss of slaves would destroy the economies of the Southern states and ruin the fortunes of individuals.

Powers of State and Federal Governments

Many representatives at the 1787 Constitutional Convention worried that a strong central government would take away the rights of the individual states. They

Paper Works

According to the chart, which state ratified the Constitution by the closest margin? Which state was the last to ratify the Constitution? Research the reasons why this state was the last to ratify. Write a brief essay explaining your findings.

Dates of Ratification of the Constitution (1787–1790)

State	Date	Votes for	Votes against
Delaware	December 7, 1787	30	0
Pennsylvania	December 12, 1787	46	23
New Jersey	December 18, 1787	38	0
Georgia	January 2, 1788	26	0
Connecticut	January 9, 1788	128	40
Massachusetts	February 6, 1788	187	168
Maryland	April 28, 1788	63	11
South Carolina	May 23, 1788	149	73
New Hampshire	June 21, 1788	57	47
Virginia	June 25, 1788	89	79
New York	June 26, 1788	30	27
North Carolina	November 21, 1789	194	77
Rhode Island	May 29, 1790	34	32

feared new taxation and unfair policies similar to the ones that they had endured under the strong British government. Many believed they were citizens of their state first and that each state deserved to govern itself in a loose union. The writers of the Constitution included three sections that dealt with slavery. The first said that the federal government would not stop

James Madison, a Constitutional Convention delegate, helped work out the issue of slave representation in the Constitution. The House of Representatives would be based on one representative for every 30,000 inhabitants of a state. A slave would count as three-fifths of a free person.

the slave trade until 1808. The second section guaranteed slaveholders the right to recover slaves who ran away to the free states. The third section dealing with slavery involved the issue of representation. Each slave would be counted as three-fifths of a person when determining the states' populations and the number of representatives each state would send to Congress. The Constitution was eventually ratified by all thirteen states, but the issue of slavery would haunt the nation for years to come.

Western Territories and States

The Mason-Dixon Line and the Ohio River separated slave and free states east of the Mississippi River. Following the Revolution, states were beginning to form west of the Mississippi. The question of whether slavery would be allowed in these states led to a number of new laws. When the Missouri Territory applied for statehood in 1818 as a slave state, some Northerners opposed this. Congress needed to work out a compromise.

In the law called the Missouri Compromise, or the Compromise of 1820, Maine was admitted as a free state and Missouri was allowed to include the practice of slavery in its state constitution. The Missouri Compromise created a balance of twelve slave states and twelve free states. Furthermore, any state that was created from the Louisiana Territory and that was situated north of the imaginary line drawn at 36 degrees 30 minutes north latitude,

Fact Finder

Use the sample outline below to create your own outline of the Compromises of 1820 and 1850. Include more details if needed. Use the outline to write an essay that explains why these laws were not effective in halting the oncoming Civil War.

I) Compromise of 1820

  a) Detail one

  b) Detail two

  c) Detail three

II) Compromise of 1850

  a) Detail one

  b) Detail two

  c) Detail three

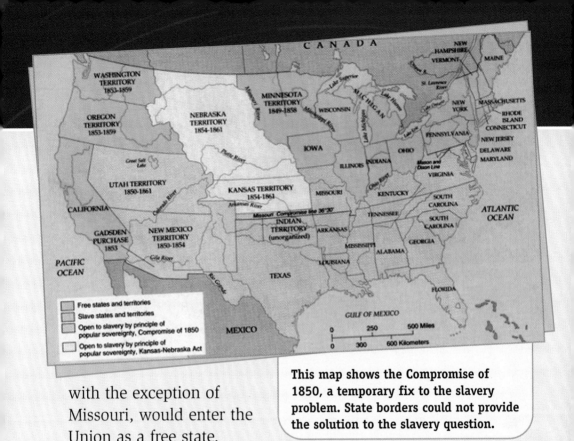

This map shows the Compromise of 1850, a temporary fix to the slavery problem. State borders could not provide the solution to the slavery question.

with the exception of Missouri, would enter the Union as a free state.

The United States won new territory after the Mexican War (1846–1848), and once again the issue of slavery in the territories arose. Kentucky senator Henry Clay proposed the Compromise of 1850, in which California was admitted as a free state, and the territories of New Mexico and Utah would be allowed to decide for themselves whether to be slave or free states. This was called popular sovereignty. Also, Washington, D.C., would prohibit slave trading, but slavery would remain legal there. A new slave law, called the Fugitive Slave Law, would be passed to make it easier for Southerners to reclaim their slaves. Because of this new law, many fugitive slaves, as well as free blacks, were taken from freedom in the North to slavery in the South. This law caused great fury among Northern abolitionists.

The Fight Against Slavery

The Fugitive Slave Law fueled the antislavery movement. One organization, the Underground Railroad, guided almost 100,000 slaves to freedom in the North. After Congress passed the Fugitive Slave Law in 1850, the Underground Railroad redoubled its efforts to help slaves escape in greater numbers, especially with the assistance of "conductors," such as the former slave Harriet Tubman and the Quaker abolitionist Levi Coffin. Frederick Douglass's autobiography, entitled *Narrative of the Life of Frederick Douglass* (published in 1845), enabled the public to read an actual account of the life of a slave. Harriet Beecher Stowe's novel *Uncle Tom's Cabin* (1852) also helped gain support for ending slavery. Southerners, angry at these antislavery books, wrote books supporting their proslavery beliefs and related stories about slaves being happier than many Northern white factory workers.

The Kansas-Nebraska Act of 1854 allowed for the organization of two new states into the Union. Under the Missouri Compromise, slavery was prohibited in Kansas and Nebraska. But the concept of popular sovereignty first seen in the Compromise of 1850 was applied by the

Paper Works

Using the map on page 11 as a guide, draw or shade a map of the United States showing the free states and slave states after the Kansas-Nebraska Act of 1854. Write a caption for your map that explains why this act helped to push the United States toward the Civil War.

This 1835 political cartoon shows an actual antislavery meeting that took place in Boston, Massachusetts. William Lloyd Garrison *(center)*, with a rope around his neck, was dragged through the streets by a mob. He printed his newspaper the *Liberator* in Boston, in which he called for the ending of slavery.

Kansas-Nebraska Act to allow those states to decide their own status. Northerners were upset by this decision because it contradicted the Compromise of 1820—no state north of 36 degrees 30 minutes could be a slave state. Nevertheless, President Franklin Pierce approved this law.

Both proslavery and antislavery voters in Kansas and Nebraska rushed to the polls to vote on the issue. Some organizations sent settlers for the purpose of voting. At one poll, only 20 out of 600 voters were residents of the state. Fighting began. The violence in Kansas increased so much that the state was nicknamed Bleeding Kansas. After two opposing congressmen's beliefs led to blows in Washington, D.C., senators began carrying weapons with them. Kansas became a free state in 1861.

A Supreme Court Decision

Dred Scott, a slave from Missouri, once again brought national attention to the slavery issue. Scott had lived with a slave owner in the free state of Illinois and the free territory of Wisconsin before being taken back to the slave state of Missouri. Scott sued for his freedom in 1846, believing that his time living in a free state would grant him the rights and privileges of U.S. citizenship. In 1857, eleven years after Scott first filed his suit, the United States Supreme Court handed down a decision against Scott in *Dred Scott v. Sandford*.

Chief Justice Roger B. Taney insisted that because blacks were not and could not be citizens of the United States, they had no right to sue. Moreover, he said that Congress had no right to ban slavery from any territories, ruling that the Missouri Compromise was unconstitutional. Dred Scott's owner still freed Scott two months later, but the country was pushed to the brink of war.

John Brown, a white farmer, was convinced from a young age that his duty was to rid the country of slavery. Brown thought that violence was the only way to complete his mission. Earlier, in 1856, he and his followers killed several

Q & A

1. What does the word "intelligence" mean in the first headline of the newspaper pictured on page 15?

2. Why do you think John Brown is not mentioned?

3. What words might cause people to worry about a future conflict?

proslavery settlers in Kansas. On October 16, 1859, he raided a federal armory in Harpers Ferry, Virginia (now West Virginia), in an attempt to get weapons for his assault and to call on slaves in the South to revolt and to help liberate fellow slaves. Brown was soon captured by Colonel Robert E. Lee and was later tried, convicted, and hanged. His story was popularized as a song often sung by Northern forces in the Civil War: "John Brown's body lies a-moldering in the ground/His soul is marching on." Brown became a hero to many who supported his attempt to end the practice of slavery.

FEARFUL AND EXCITING INTELLIGENCE.

NEGRO INSURRECTION AT HARPER'S FERRY.

Extensive Negro Conspiracy in Virginia and Maryland.

Seizure of the United States Arsenal by the Insurrectionists.

Arms Taken and Sent into the Interior.

The Bridge Fortified and Defended by Cannon.

Trains Fired into and Stopped---Several Persons Killed---Telegraph Wires Cut---Contributions Levied on the Citizens.

Troops Despatched Against the Insurgents from Washington and Baltimore,

&c.., &c.., &c.

The *New York Herald* printed these headlines about the raid on Harpers Ferry on October 18, 1859.

The Presidential Election of 1860

As the presidential election of 1860 neared, the nation was tense. The slavery question had brought change to the political parties as well. The Republican Party had formed in 1854 on the platform that slavery was wrong and new territories should be free states. Some members of the Whig and Democratic parties joined the new party. The remainder of the Democratic Party split into two parties: Southern Democrats (proslavery) and Northern Democrats (for popular sovereignty).

Abraham Lincoln, from Illinois, ran as the presidential candidate for the Republican Party. Stephen A. Douglas, the senator behind the Kansas-Nebraska Act, ran for the Northern Democrats. Vice President John Breckinridge ran for the Southern Democrats. In addition, a third party, made up mostly of Whigs and members of the anti-immigrant American Party, or Know-Nothing Party, called itself the Constitutional Union Party and supported former senator John Bell of Tennessee.

The Democrats split their votes, whereas all Republican votes went to Abraham Lincoln. He won a majority of the electoral votes in the North, which

Get Graphic

Look at the chart that shows the presidential election results of 1860. The pie charts show the results of the electoral and popular votes. Explain in a well-developed essay the difference between the results and why this difference may have been significant to the nation's people.

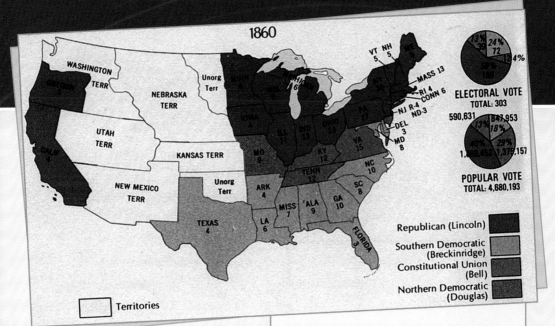

This map and the accompanying pie charts show the results of the electoral and popular vote during the U.S. presidential election in 1860.

was enough to win the election even without votes from the South. However, Lincoln won only about 40 percent of the popular vote. He was not even on the tickets of many Southern states. Some Southern states, led by South Carolina, decided that they would secede from the Union before Lincoln even took office. They thought that Lincoln would attack slavery in the South, and they decided to take action before he had a chance to do this. The Southern secessionists believed that states had the right to leave the Union. Lincoln disagreed. He believed that the Union was perpetual and that he had fairly won the election.

Secession

Abraham Lincoln was elected president in November 1860. South Carolina was the first state to secede from the Union on December 20. Mississippi, Florida, Alabama, Georgia, Louisiana, and Texas soon followed. The seven states formed the Confederate States of America. They met in February 1861 and elected Jefferson Davis as their provisional president. The structure of the Confederate government mirrored that of the Union government. In March, the secessionist states ratified a constitution similar to the U.S. Constitution. However, this document guaranteed the right of slaveholders to take their slaves into the territories.

Fact Finder

Examine the newspaper pictured on page 19. Use it to answer the following questions:

1. What is the most important idea that the *Charleston Mercury* newspaper wished to represent?
2. Why do you think this?
3. How many people voted against secession according to the paper?
4. Why is this detail important?
5. If you were reading this newspaper in 1860, what questions would be left unanswered?

The first conflict between the Confederacy and the Union took place at Fort Sumter, a federal fort in South Carolina. When the Union commander of the fort asked Lincoln for more weapons and supplies, Lincoln sent only supplies. But the Confederate forces refused to let the supplies into the fort and decided to open fire. So began the Civil War.

The first shots were fired at 4:30 AM on April 12, 1861. Arkansas, North Carolina, Tennessee, and Virginia decided to leave the Union. Four slave states remained in the Union: Missouri, Kentucky, Maryland, and Delaware. In addition, the western part of Virginia remained in the Union and formed a new state in 1863.

CHARLESTON MERCURY

EXTRA:

Passed unanimously at 1.15 o'clock, P. M., December 20th, 1860.

AN ORDINANCE

To dissolve the Union between the State of South Carolina and other States united with her under the compact entitled " The Constitution of the United States of America."

We, the People of the State of South Carolina, in Convention assembled, do declare and ordain, and it is hereby declared and ordained,

That the Ordinance adopted by us in Convention, on the twenty-third day of May, in the year of our Lord one thousand seven hundred and eighty-eight, whereby the Constitution of the United States of America was ratified, and also, all Acts and parts of Acts of the General Assembly of this State, ratifying amendments of the said Constitution, are hereby repealed ; and that the union now subsisting between South Carolina and other States, under the name of "The United States of America," is hereby dissolved.

THE UNION IS DISSOLVED!

The *Charleston Mercury* on December 20, 1860, announced the passage of South Carolina's ordinance to dissolve the Union.

Preparations

The conflict many had feared had begun. Each side prepared itself for war. When the resources of the two sides are compared, it is understandable why many in the North thought the war would not last long. The population of the North was about 22 million people, including 500,000 slaves. Nine million people lived in the South, including more than 3.5 million slaves. Eleven states were part of the Confederacy at this point, whereas twenty-three states and the existing territories fought for the Union.

The South depended on Northern and European goods and materials. In 1860, the South imported $331 million of resources, while the North, which had more highly developed industries than the South, imported only $31 million. This dependence would later cause a problem for the South. The South also hoped that

Think Tank

Form a group of several students. Your group should create two bar graphs illustrating two differences between Northern and Southern resources, such as the graphs shown on page 21. Choose one category that is discussed in the text and one that is not. Research this category on the Internet or at the library. Use your graphs to write a paragraph of comparison discussing how these resources gave one side an advantage over the other.

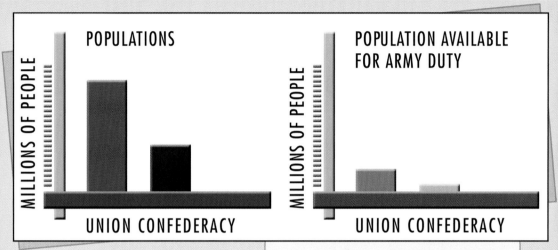

These bar graphs show the number of men available for duty in the army in the North and the South compared to the population living in both regions.

Europeans who relied on Southern cotton would aid in the war. This aid would never come.

Both sides called for volunteers to fight for their cause. The United States Army at this time was made up of about 16,000 men, mostly from the North. Rather than the federal government calling for troops, each state organized groups of soldiers. Each volunteer received an amount of money. A few simply took the money and deserted the army. But a great number, including many immigrants, jumped at the chance to fight for a noble cause. Some women even wore disguises so that they could fight. Loreta Janeta Velazquez claimed to have fought in at least four battles using the name Harry T. Buford.

First Battle in the East (1861)

Fighting in the Civil War was divided into two major fronts. The Union strategy involved surrounding the Confederate states with a naval blockade, trying to capture the Confederate capital of Richmond, and attacking down the Mississippi River to cut the Confederacy in two. Whereas the Union had to defeat the Confederacy to win, the Confederacy just had to force the Union to give up. This led to different strategies. In the east, most of the battles took place between the two capitals, Washington and Richmond. In the west, the battles were fought in Kentucky, Tennessee, and Mississippi with some other battles being fought west of the Mississippi River.

The first commander of the Army of the Potomac, as the Union force in the east was called, was General Irvin McDowell. In July 1861, McDowell led his army to Manassas, Virginia. His plan was to attack the Confederate forces, headed by General Pierre Beauregard. Unknown to McDowell, Confederate general Joseph Johnston and his army escaped Union

Q & A

Use the map on page 23 and the text to answer the following questions:

1. In which direction was McDowell's Union army traveling?
   a) Northwest
   b) Southwest
   c) Southeast
   d) Northeast

2. About how far was Manassas Junction from Washington, D.C.?
   a) 30 miles
   b) 10 miles
   c) 50 miles
   d) 5 miles

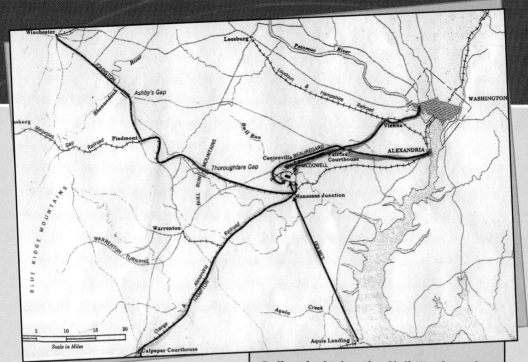

forces in the Shenandoah Valley and traveled by railroad to help Beauregard and the other Confederates. The Union army of about 35,000 troops met the Confederate army of about 32,000 soldiers on July 21, 1861.

Railroads during the Civil War brought supplies, information, and soldiers to battlefields. They brought Johnston and Hampton's Confederate soldiers to the First Battle of Bull Run. The United States Military Railroads, created in February 1862, took over the operation of captured Confederate railroads.

Neither side had devoted much time to training its soldiers. The Northern troops, in particular, became confused and panicked before retreating. The South won this battle with the help of Confederate commander Thomas J. Jackson, whose force was so unyielding he became known as Stonewall Jackson. The Confederate victory was a sign that the war would not be won quickly. This battle would later be known as the First Battle of Bull Run by the North. The South called it the First Battle of Manassas.

The Peninsula Battles (May–July 1862)

After the Union troops' failure at the First Battle of Bull Run, Lincoln appointed General George McClellan as leader of the Army of the Potomac. McClellan's aim was to capture Richmond. He spent much time organizing and training his men, hoping not to repeat the mistakes of the Battle of Bull Run. McClellan finally assembled his force of 100,000 on the Virginia peninsula between the York and James rivers in May 1862.

McClellan took more than two months to lead his troops from the tip of the peninsula to Richmond. On May 31, about 6 miles (9.7 kilometers) away from Richmond, he was met by the Confederate forces of General Johnston. The Union forces won the first major confrontation there, at the Battle of Fair Oaks (Seven Pines). Johnston was wounded in the battle and President Jefferson Davis replaced him with Robert E. Lee, who became leader of the renamed Army of Northern Virginia.

Get Graphic

The battles between McClellan's Union forces and the Confederate forces were known as the Peninsula Campaign. According to the map, which bodies of water transported McClellan's army to the peninsula?

a) Potomac River
b) Pacific Ocean
c) Chesapeake Bay
d) Delaware Bay

General McClellan's Peninsula Campaign was a plan in which the Union's navy would transport McClellan's troops to the peninsula between the James and York rivers, and would protect the army's flanks as it marched toward Richmond. However, the Union plan failed.

McClellan wanted more troops before he pushed his army to capture Richmond. But Stonewall Jackson kept Union forces in the Shenandoah Valley busy and so prevented them from being sent to McClellan's aid. Lee and Jackson joined forces at the Seven Days' Battles, which began on June 26. McClellan's army was pushed back from its position on the Chickahominy River, saving Richmond from Union occupation. McClellan moved back up the James River to Northern Virginia to prepare to start a new campaign with the addition of Union general John Pope's soldiers.

The Eastern Battles Continue (August–December 1862)

General Robert E. Lee did not wait for McClellan's Union force to join Pope and his troops in Manassas, Virginia. He sent Stonewall Jackson to attack Pope before McClellan could reach him. Pope's men and Jackson's forces fought on August 29, 1862. McClellan's troops finally arrived, but Lee and General James Longstreet also brought reinforcements. The Union lost the Second Battle of Bull Run.

Lee took his Confederate soldiers into the Union border state of Maryland, where he would make the first attempt to capture territory in a Union state. On September 13, McClellan's scouts found Lee's plans wrapped around cigars at an abandoned camp. McClellan, who was often accused of inaction, waited several days to attack, allowing Lee and Jackson to unite forces. On September 17, the two forces (about 75,000 Union troops and 38,000 Confederate troops) fought the deadliest battle at Antietam (called Sharpsburg by the South) in the deadliest war in U.S. history. The total number of casualties— those who died, were wounded, or were miss-

Think Tank

Pair up with another learner. Review the important eastern battle dates in 1862. Have one person write down important events and their dates. Have the other person use the information to construct a timeline that shows the order of events.

More Americans died in the one-day Battle of Antietam on September 17, 1862, than died during the entire American Revolution.

ing—was about 26,000 soldiers. After the battle, Lee retreated, making this a slim Northern victory despite the great loss of life.

Because McClellan had allowed the retreat of the weakened Confederate forces, Lincoln replaced him with Ambrose Burnside as commander of the Army of the Potomac. Burnside took the Union forces to meet Lee in Fredericksburg, Virginia. Lee's troops were stationed in the hills of Marye's Heights, Virginia, waiting for the Union's attack. The Union, missing the protection of the hills, suffered great losses there on December 13, 1862, at the Battle of Fredericksburg. There were almost 13,000 Union casualties. Five thousand Confederates were killed or missing. Burnside stepped down as Union commander.

Army Conditions

One year into the Civil War, there was a shortage of volunteers in both the Union and Confederate forces. Both sides set up drafts to enlist men of a certain age range into the army. In 1863, the North drafted men from ages 20 through 45 for three years of service. In the South, the age range changed from 18 to 35 in 1862, to 17 through 50 in 1864. The South had a smaller population and had to expand the age range to obtain more troops.

In both the North and South, a man who was drafted could pay another man to serve his term of three years. In the South, the law also exempted people who held certain jobs, such as clergymen, apothecaries, and white men on any plantation with a ratio of at least twenty slaves per white man. Northern and Southern soldiers complained that these rules made this "a rich man's war and a poor man's fight." Some angry draftees led riots, such as those in New York City in July 1863. They burned buildings, and nearly 100 people

Word Works

The draft is sometimes called conscription. The process of conscription was used in later wars as well. Explain why some people believed that the Civil War was "a rich man's war and a poor man's fight." Explain why some might believe this was true.

The number of Northern hospitals, like the one pictured here, rose from 16 before the war to more than 350 by 1865. The South built more than 150. Women were crucial in the care of the wounded. Clara Barton *(inset)*, who became the North's head of nurses during the war, would later found the American Red Cross.

were killed over a period of three days. The draft was effective, however. By the end of the war, the North had more than 2 million soldiers and sailors. The Confederacy had about 850,000 soldiers and sailors, but by 1865, this number dwindled to about 200,000.

Shameful conditions in the army led to a 10 percent desertion rate on each side. Soldiers were poorly paid and had insufficient clothing and food. Technological advances in weaponry led to many more deaths on both sides. In some battles, 25 percent of an army was killed.

Blacks in the Civil War

As a way of trying to bring the war to a close, following the Battle of Antietam in September 1862, President Lincoln issued his Emancipation Proclamation. Many Northerners argued that the war was about slavery and that the president should abolish slavery. Lincoln had been considering how to do this. With the Antietam victory, he could go through with the proclamation without it looking like an act of desperation. The proclamation stated that on January 1, 1863, all slaves in the Confederate states would be free. Lincoln did not order that all slaves in all states were to be freed. The Union border states that allowed slavery included Kentucky, Maryland, Delaware, Missouri, and the new territory of West Virginia. Lincoln feared that freeing all the slaves in the nation would cause these border states to join the Confederate cause. However, freeing the slaves in the Confederate states could weaken the Southern economy and encourage blacks to help the Northern effort. At first, this proclamation did nothing, but as the Northern armies

Fact Finder

Review the information in this section. Write a short essay describing the Northern and Southern troops' views of blacks during the Civil War. Explain why these views might have changed as the war stretched over several years.

The 54th Massachusetts Infantry was comprised of 600 free blacks, among them sons of the abolitionist Frederick Douglass. It won glory and admiration in a battle at Fort Wagner, South Carolina, on July 18, 1863. Sergeant William Carney was the first black to receive a Congressional Medal of Honor for his bravery.

moved through the South, the slaves were freed. For many Southerners, the Emancipation Proclamation only strengthened their resolve to fight for Southern independence.

With the Emancipation Proclamation, President Lincoln also allowed blacks to serve in the Union army. Previously, they had only been allowed to serve in the navy. At first, blacks mainly took jobs as cooks, scouts, and spies. Later, about 180,000 blacks were counted as soldiers in the Northern army; many were slaves who had escaped from the South. Although many blacks showed leadership qualities and bravery, only about 100 became officers. They repeatedly proved their heroic qualities, even in the face of discrimination in the army.

Chancellorsville and Gettysburg (1863)

In the spring of 1863, the new commander of the eastern Union forces, Joseph Hooker, moved to attack Lee at Chancellorsville, Virginia, on April 27, 1863. However, Lee's forces of 60,000 managed to break the Union troops numbering more than 110,000 with the skillful direction of their commander. Lee split his army into some smaller groups so that he was able to attack at several different points. Hooker was forced to retreat on May 4. Lee suffered a great loss in the accidental death of Stonewall Jackson soon after, when Jackson's troops were mistaken for Union soldiers, and Jackson was shot by Confederates.

General Lee and his forces now decided to invade the North. They marched through Maryland and into Pennsylvania in June 1863. The Army of the Potomac pursued Lee. The two armies met at Gettysburg, Pennsylvania. By now, General George Meade commanded the Union army. The fighting began by chance, as a Confederate group searching for shoes ran into a Union force.

Think Tank

Find a copy of the Gettysburg Address (or go to this Web site for a transcription: http://www.loc.gov/exhibits/gadd/gatr1.html). Form a group of three learners. Have one student read the Gettysburg Address aloud. After each sentence, discuss the meaning of Lincoln's words. Have a student write, in outline form, the meaning of Lincoln's words. After you have reviewed your outline, discuss what Lincoln hoped to convey to the nation with his speech. Write an essay describing why Lincoln's speech is still considered historically significant.

There are only five manuscript copies of the Gettysburg Address written by Abraham Lincoln. The one pictured here is the one now housed in the Lincoln room of the White House.

On July 1, the battle began between the Northern army of 85,000 and the Southern army of 65,000. The fight lasted three days. On July 3, Lee ordered General George Pickett to lead 13,000 Confederates to break the Union's center formation. Only half of the Confederates survived this attack, which would be called Pickett's Charge. Lee withdrew into Virginia, never again to march into Union territory. Both sides suffered great losses in men, more than 50,000 were killed or wounded. A cemetery was dedicated in Gettysburg by the Union to those who had given their lives in the battle. At the ceremony, Abraham Lincoln delivered what is known as the Gettysburg Address, in which he honored the dead and assured the public that the Union and the Republican principles that it stood for would survive.

Battles West of the Appalachians (1862–1864)

Many conflicts took place west of the Appalachian Mountains, focusing on the capture of waterways, which carried Confederate supplies. Under the command of Union general Henry Halleck, General Ulysses S. Grant and his forces took two Confederate forts—Fort Henry in Kentucky and Fort Donelson in Tennessee. After these conquests in February 1862, the Union controlled Kentucky and part of Tennessee.

On orders, Grant traveled down the Tennessee River to join forces with General Don Carlos Buell. The combined army was to move down the Mississippi. Before Grant and Buell could meet, Confederate generals Albert Johnston and Pierre Beauregard's army attacked Grant's force on April 6, 1862, in Pittsburg Landing, Tennessee. Grant's men fought until reinforcements arrived the next day. The Southern forces retreated to Mississippi. About one out of every four men was killed at the Battle of Shiloh. Some in the North called Grant a "butcher" because he lost so many soldiers. Lincoln, though, admired Grant's courage.

Word Works

The word "siege" is related to the Latin word *sedere*, which means "to sit." In a siege, a group of soldiers surrounds a city, sitting and waiting for its residents to surrender. What are the advantages of a siege over combat? What are the disadvantages?

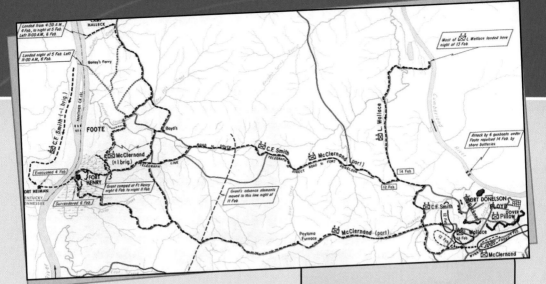

The Union captured New Orleans, Louisiana, in May 1862, and Corinth, Mississippi. Confederate general Braxton Bragg was forced south as the

new Union western commander General William Rosencrans defeated him in Murfreesboro, Tennessee, in the Battle of Stones River. Rosencrans's forces were defeated in Chickamauga, Tennessee, in September 1863. This would be the South's last major victory.

Grant then masterminded a siege of Vicksburg, Mississippi, leading to the city's surrender on July 4, 1863, a day after the Union victory at Gettysburg. The siege lasted forty-eight days, causing near starvation for the town and its defenders. Grant gained control of the Mississippi River and was given the command of all western Union forces. With the Vicksburg victory, the Confederacy was cut in two. After Grant and General George Thomas won Chattanooga, Tennessee, on November 25, the South realized it was losing land and soldiers. Also, because of the Union blockade, it badly needed supplies from overseas.

A Unified Union Army (1864–1865)

By March 1864, Lincoln put all Union forces in the hands of General Grant. Grant set out to destroy Lee's army and to capture Richmond, the Confederate capital.

Under Grant's direction, the eastern Army of the Potomac, led by General Meade, moved south to defeat Lee and to capture Richmond. Their first encounter on May 5 was in a forested area of northern Virginia called the Wilderness. Both sides suffered major losses with no clear victor in the battle.

Get Graphic

Examine the table on the next page. Use it to answer the following questions:

1. On what date was the Union army at its largest?
    a) January 1862
    b) January 1863
    c) January 1864
    d) January 1865

2. On what date was the Confederate army at its smallest?
    a) January 1862
    b) January 1863
    c) January 1864
    d) January 1865

Estimated Number of Soldiers in the Union and Confederate Armies		
Date	Union	Confederacy
January 1862	527,200	258,700
January 1863	698,800	304,000
January 1864	611,300	278,000
January 1865	621,000	196,800

Grant and Lee met again at the Battle of Spotsylvania Court House on May 8, and still there was no clear victory for either side. Lee's army raced to Cold Harbor, where soldiers dug trenches and killed more than 6,000 Union men. Not until Grant's men surrounded Petersburg, the rail center that provided supplies to Richmond, did Grant gain an advantage over Lee. The Siege of Petersburg began on June 20, 1864.

In the South, Grant ordered General William T. Sherman to capture Atlanta, Georgia. Sherman's large army met little resistance from the smaller forces of Confederate Joseph Johnston. Confederate commander John Hood tried to strike before Sherman entered Atlanta but failed. Sherman gained Atlanta on September 2, 1864. His men began a march through Georgia and South Carolina, burning large areas of Atlanta and Columbia. Sherman hoped these measures would make the South surrender.

Lee's forces at Petersburg tried to escape at the end of March 1865. Lee's attempt to combine forces with other Confederate troops was blocked by the Union. Lee had no choice but to surrender and to allow Richmond to fall.

Beyond the American Civil War

On April 9, 1865, Robert E. Lee and Ulysses S. Grant met at Appomattox Court House in Virginia. Grant offered the terms of the surrender. The Confederate soldiers were allowed to keep their personal possessions and were offered food. Lee accepted these terms. This generous treatment of "the enemy" was important in healing the split between the North and South. Confederate armies in North Carolina, Alabama, Mississippi, and Indian Territory (now Oklahoma) surrendered weeks later. As no formal Confederacy existed after the fall of Richmond, the surrenders of these armies marked the end of the war.

Lincoln turned his thoughts to reuniting and rebuilding the nation. The lands of the South were especially damaged. Families mourned their fathers and sons—more than 620,000 soldiers were killed. The period of rebuilding the South after the war is called Reconstruction. However, five days after the meeting at Appomattox Court House, Abraham Lincoln was assassinated. The country was in shock. Many were unsure if the Southern forces would rise up again, now that the Union leader was dead. But most in the South just wanted peace.

Think Tank

Gather a group of three or four students. Lincoln preferred the term "reconciliation" for the period of Reconstruction. What government policies could have made this transition process successful? Write down your ideas. Then research the government policies that were in place during this period.

This 1866 illustration shows former slaves celebrating the abolition of slavery in the District of Columbia after President Lincoln's Emancipation Proclamation.

Andrew Johnson assumed the presidency, and he continued the process of rebuilding the United States. The South was not allowed to rejoin the Union until it had made some reforms, including accepting the end of slavery. Congress passed the Thirteenth Amendment in January 1865, ending slavery in the United States. Blacks were free, but they did not yet have equal rights. To aid them, several laws were passed in the first few postwar years, including the Civil Rights Act of 1866 and the Fourteenth Amendment to the Constitution. Much death and destruction resulted from the American Civil War. But the end also marked a new beginning for millions of former slaves. Lincoln had succeeded in his task—the Union had been preserved.

Timeline

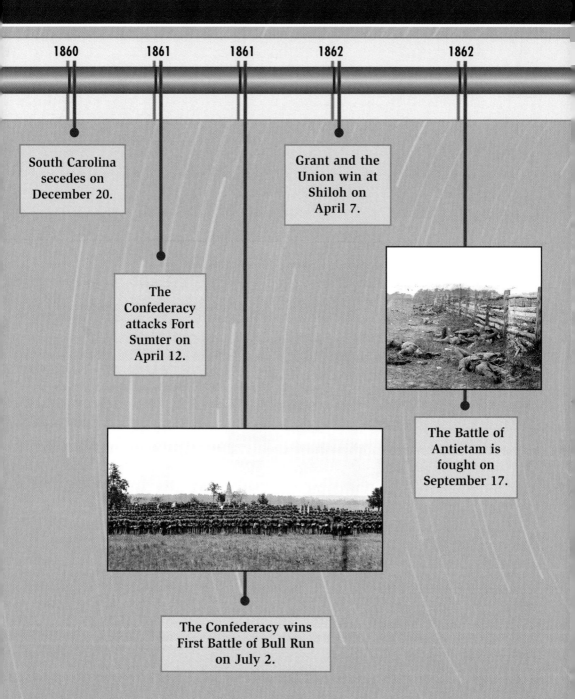

1860   1861   1861   1862   1862

South Carolina secedes on December 20.

Grant and the Union win at Shiloh on April 7.

The Confederacy attacks Fort Sumter on April 12.

The Battle of Antietam is fought on September 17.

The Confederacy wins First Battle of Bull Run on July 2.

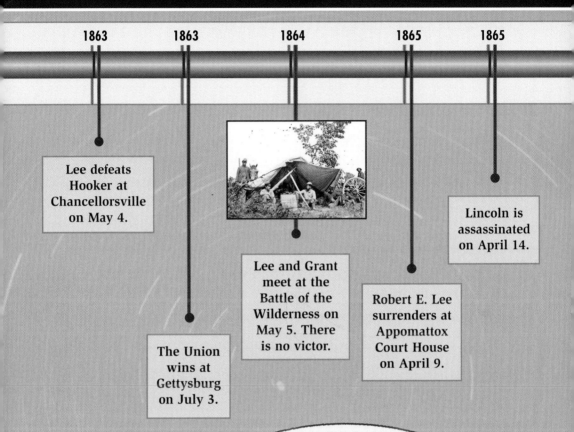

| 1863 | 1863 | 1864 | 1865 | 1865 |

Lee defeats Hooker at Chancellorsville on May 4.

Lincoln is assassinated on April 14.

Lee and Grant meet at the Battle of the Wilderness on May 5. There is no victor.

Robert E. Lee surrenders at Appomattox Court House on April 9.

The Union wins at Gettysburg on July 3.

Get with the Times

Look over the events of the American Civil War in the timeline. Answer the following questions:

✓ When was the last major Confederate victory at Chancellorsville, Virginia?

✓ When did Lee surrender?

✓ How much time passed between Lee's surrender and Lincoln's assassination?

Graphic Organizers in Action

Problem/Solution Outline

Problem: New states will disrupt the balance between slave and free states.

Solution 1: Missouri Compromise (Compromise of 1820)	**Result 1:** Admits Maine as free state and Missouri as slave state
Solution 2: Compromise of 1850	**Result 2:** Admits California; allows New Mexico and Utah to decide own status; allows Fugitive Slave Law
Solution 3: Kansas-Nebraska Act of 1854	**Result 3:** Allows Kansas and Nebraska to vote on the issue; leads to violence in Kansas

End Results: Slave and free states are temporarily balanced, but this issue and other factors push the North and the South into civil war in 1861.

5 Ws + 1 H Chart

Who: Union general Ulysses S. Grant and Confederate general Robert E. Lee

When: April 9, 1865

What: Agreed to end war

Where: Appomattox Court House, Virginia

Why: To discuss the terms of the surrender of Lee's army

How: In return for a peaceful surrender, Grant gave Lee's soldiers badly needed food, permitted them to return home to their families, and allowed them to keep many of their personal possessions. Lee's army was the largest and most important military force of the Confederacy. Its surrender would mark the end of the Civil War.

Cluster Chart

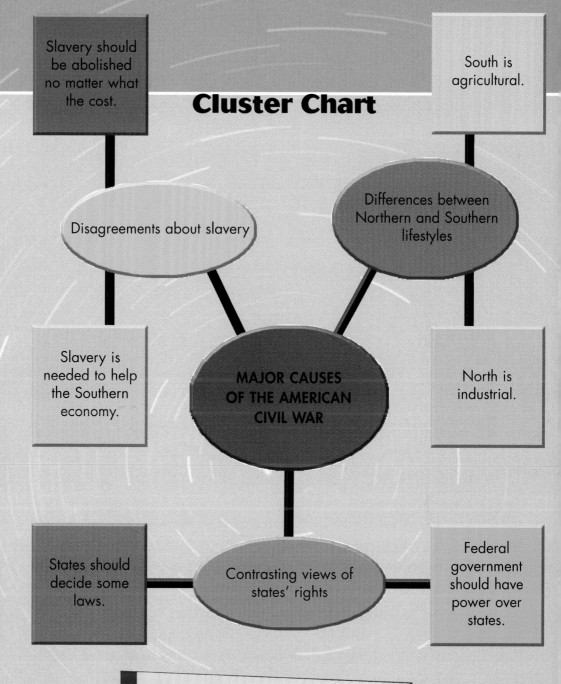

Slavery should be abolished no matter what the cost.

South is agricultural.

Disagreements about slavery

Differences between Northern and Southern lifestyles

Slavery is needed to help the Southern economy.

MAJOR CAUSES OF THE AMERICAN CIVIL WAR

North is industrial.

States should decide some laws.

Contrasting views of states' rights

Federal government should have power over states.

Q & A

Examine the graphic organizers on these pages. Use one of the organizers as a guide to explain the presidential election of 1860 and its results.

43

Glossary

aggressive (uh-GREH-siv) Marked by a willingness to fight.

armory (AR-muh-ree) A place to store weapons and military equipment.

blockade (blah-KAYD) The blocking of troops and supplies to an enemy area by a warring group or nation.

casualty (KA-zhul-tee) A military person lost through death, wounds, injury, sickness, capture, or imprisonment, or by being missing in action.

compromise (KOM-pruh-myz) A settlement of differences in which each side gives up something to come to a mutual agreement.

conductor (kun-DUK-ter) A guide.

confederate (kun-FEH-duh-ret) A member of an alliance.

draft (DRAFT) A method for selecting people for military service.

electoral vote (ee-LEK-tuh-rul VOHT) A vote of a member of the electoral college, a group of people appointed to elect the president and vice president of the United States.

emancipation (ih-man-sih-PAY-shun) The act of freeing a person from the control or power of someone else.

Fugitive Slave Law (FYOO-jeh-tiv SLAYV LAW) A law passed by the U.S. Congress in 1850 as part of the Compromise of 1850 between Southern slaveholders and Northern antislavery supporters. The law called for citizens to help in returning fugitive slaves, and it took away an escaped slave's right to a trial by jury. Instead, the escaped slave would have his or her case handled by special commissioners.

peninsula (peh-NIN-suh-luh) An area of land nearly surrounded by water.

platform (PLAT-form) The principles and policies on which a political party or candidate stands.

popular sovereignty (PAH-pyoo-lar SAH-ver-en-tee) A pre–Civil War doctrine that asserted the right of the people living in a newly organized territory to decide by vote of their territorial legislature whether slavery would be permitted there.

reconciliation (reh-kuhn-sih-lee-AY-shun) Restoring a friendship or bond.

Reconstruction (ree-kun-STRUHK-shun) After the American Civil War, the rebuilding of the government and land of the states that seceded from the Union.

siege (SEEJ) A military blockade of a city or other fortification to force its surrender.

Web Sites

Due to the changing nature of Internet links, the Rosen Publishing Group, Inc., has developed an online list of Web sites related to the subject of this book. This site is updated regularly. Please use this link to access the list:

http://www.rosenlinks.com/ctah/iacw

For Further Reading

Bolotin, Norman. *The Civil War A to Z: A Young Readers' Guide to Over 100 People, Places, and Points of Interest*. New York, NY: Dutton Children's Books, 2002.

Freedman, Russell. *Lincoln: A Photobiography*. Boston, MA: Clarion Books, 1989.

Ward, Geoffrey C., Ric Burns, and Ken Burns. *The Civil War: An Illustrated History*. New York, NY: Alfred A. Knopf, Inc., 1990.

Woodhead, Henry, ed. *Civil War Battle Atlas*. Alexandria, VA: Time-Life Books, 1996.

Index

A

abolitionists, 11
Antietam, Battle of, 26–27, 30
Appomattox Court House,
    Virginia, 38
Army of the Potomac, 22, 27, 32, 36

B

Beauregard, Pierre, 22, 23, 34
blacks in military, 31
Brown, John, 14–15

C

Civil War
  end of, 38
  reasons for, 5
  results of, 4–5, 39
  start of, 19, 22
Compromise of 1850, 11, 12
Confederate States of America
  formation of, 18
  population of, 20
  surrender of, 37
  war strategy of, 22
Constitutional Convention, 6, 7, 8–9

D

Davis, Jefferson, 18, 24
drafts, military, 28–29

E

Emancipation Proclamation, 30–31

F

First Battle of Bull Run, 23, 24
Fugitive Slave Law, 11, 12

G

Gettysburg, Battle of, 32–33, 35
Gettysburg Address, 33

Grant, Ulysses S., 34–35, 36, 37, 38

J

Jackson, Thomas J. "Stonewall," 23,
    25, 26, 32
Jefferson, Thomas, 7
Johnson, Andrew, 39
Johnston, Joseph, 22, 24, 37

K

Kansas-Nebraska Act, 12–13, 16

L

Lee, Robert E., 15, 24, 26, 27, 32, 33,
    36, 37, 38
Lincoln, Abraham, 19, 24, 35, 36,
    38, 39
  assassination of, 38
  delivers Gettysburg Address, 33
  elected president, 16–17, 18
  issues Emancipation Proclamation,
    30, 31

M

McClellan, George, 24, 25, 26, 27
Meade, George, 32, 36
Missouri Compromise, 10, 12, 13, 14

P

Pope, John, 25, 26
presidential election of 1860, 16–17

R

Reconstruction, 38
Revolutionary War, 6, 10

S

Scott, Dred, 14
slavery
  Constitution and, 9, 39

About the Author

Therese Shea has a deep interest in the Civil War and its artifacts and legacy. She earned a BA degree in English from Providence College in Rhode Island, and an MA degree in English education from the State University of New York–Buffalo. She has taught high school English and currently writes and edits science, history, and math books and curricular materials in Buffalo, New York.

Photo credits: Cover (left), p. 9 © Getty Images; cover (right), pp. 5, 7, 13, 31 © Bettmann/Corbis; pp. 11, 17, 23, 25, 35 © Perry-Castañeda Library Map Collection/Historical Maps of the Americas/The University of Texas at Austin; pp. 15, 19, 40 (left and right), 41 © courtesy of the Library of Congress; p. 21 © Nelson Sá; pp. 27, 29 (inset), 39 © Corbis; p. 29 © Medford Historical Society Collection/Corbis; p. 33 © Todd Gipstein/Corbis.

Designer: Nelson Sá; Editor: Kathy Kuhtz Campbell
Photo Researcher: Nelson Sá